DAY OF DOOM

TONY BRADMAN   JAKE HILL

EDGE
W
FRANKLIN WATTS

LONDON•SYDNEY

Franklin Watts
First published in Great Britain in 2019 by The Watts Publishing Group

Text copyright © Tony Bradman 2019
Illustration copyright © The Watts Publishing Group 2019

Executive Editor: Adrian Cole
Project Editor: Katie Woolley
Designer: Cathryn Gilbert
Illustrations: Jake Hill

HB ISBN 978 1 4451 5630 9
PB ISBN 978 1 4451 5631 6
Library ebook ISBN 978 1 4451 6359 8

Printed in China

MIX
Paper from
responsible sources
FSC
www.fsc.org   FSC® C104740

Franklin Watts
An imprint of
Hachette Children's Group
Part of The Watts Publishing Group
Carmelite House
50 Victoria Embankment
London EC4Y 0DZ

An Hachette UK Company
www.hachette.co.uk

www.franklinwatts.co.uk

Layla   Jayden   Caleb

They are…

7

Layla battles the volcano but nothing seems to work.

She is running out of ideas.

"This isn't working!" said Layla. "Any ideas, Caleb?"

"Try plugging it!" shouted Caleb.

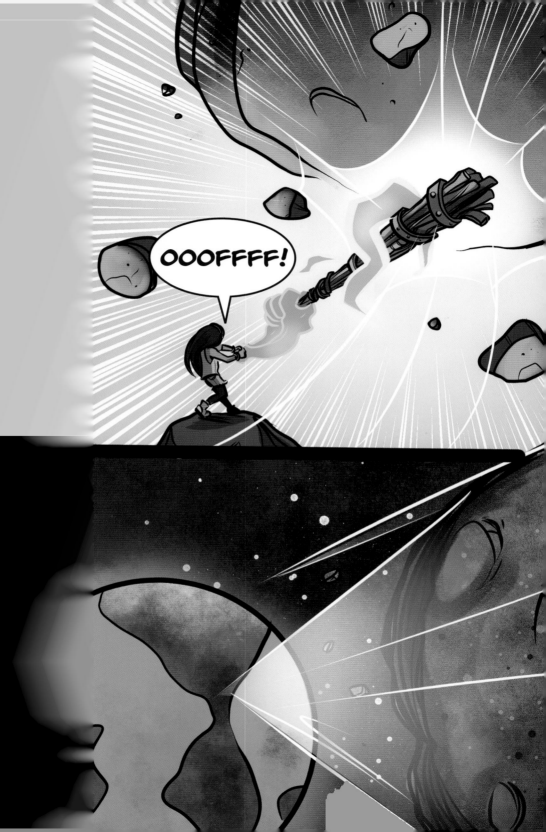